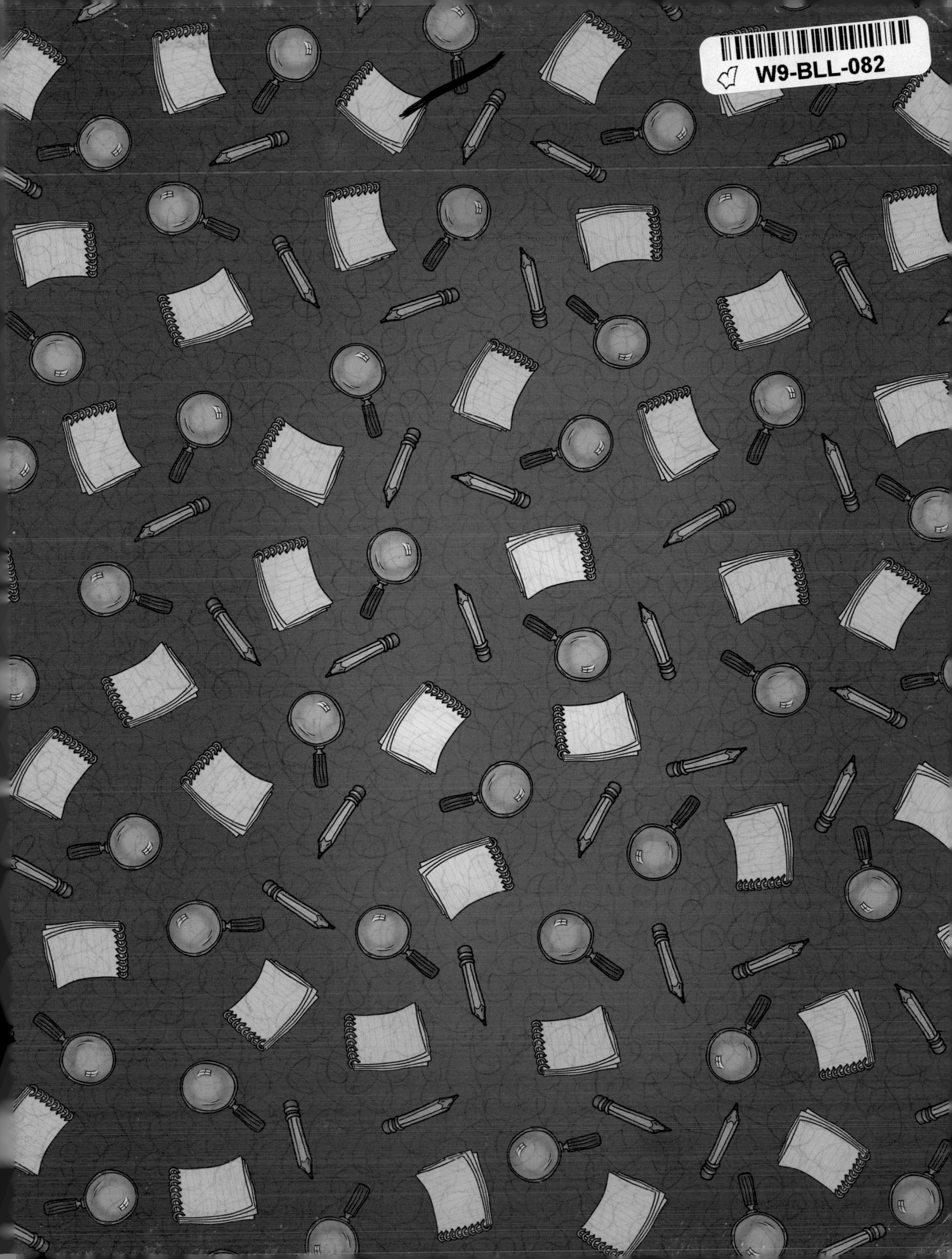
W9-BLL-082

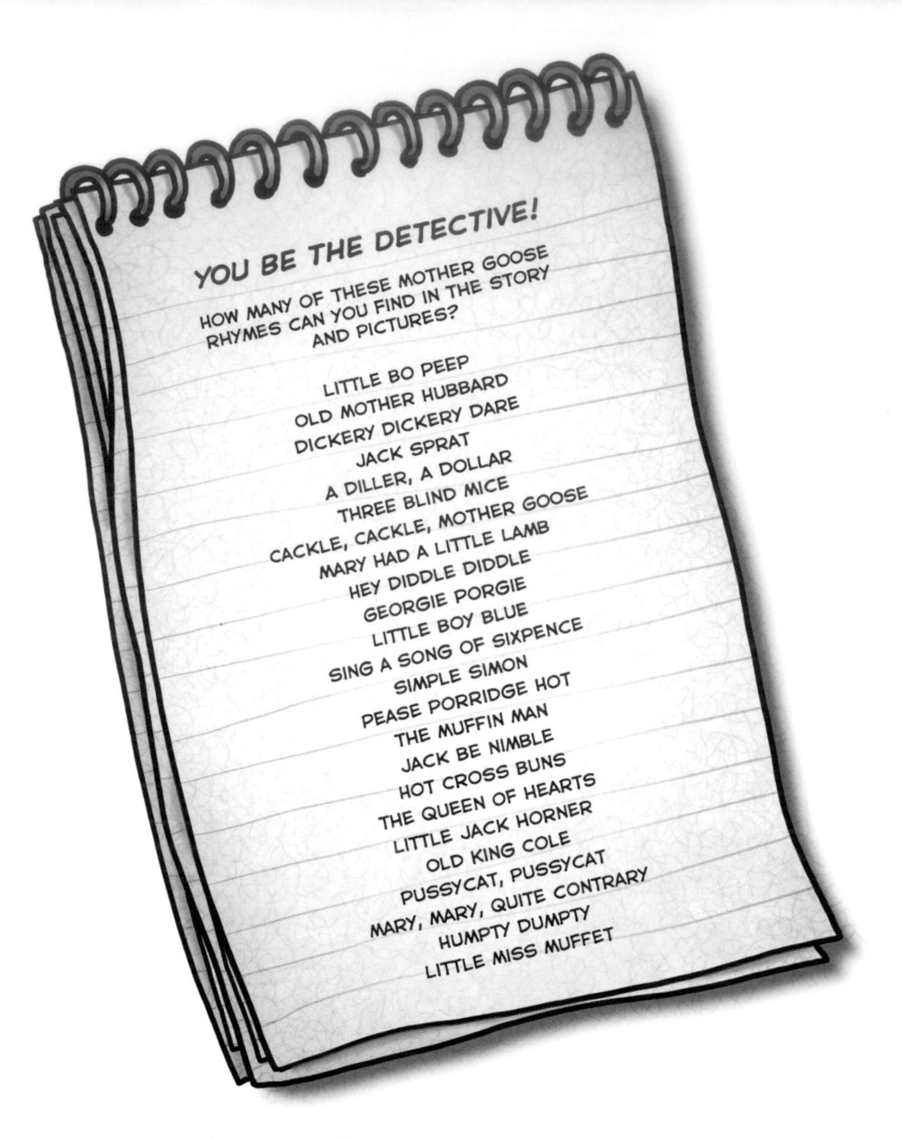

LIBRARY OF CONGRESS CATALOGING-IN-PUBLICATION DATA
METZGER, STEVE.
DETECTIVE BLUE / BY STEVE METZGER ; ILLUSTRATED BY TEDD ARNOLD. – 1ST ED.
P. CM.
SUMMARY: WITH THE HELP OF HIS NURSERY RHYME FRIENDS, LITTLE BOY BLUE,
WHO NOW RUNS A DETECTIVE AGENCY, SOLVES THE MYSTERY OF THE MISSING MISS MUFFET.
ISBN 978-0-545-17286-8
1. GRAPHIC NOVELS. [1. GRAPHIC NOVELS. 2. CHARACTERS IN LITERATURE–FICTION.
3. NURSERY RHYMES–FICTION. 4. DETECTIVES–FICTION. 5. MYSTERY AND DETECTIVE STORIES.]
I. ARNOLD, TEDD, ILL. II. TITLE.
PZ7.7.M48DE 2011
741.5'973–DC22
2010025813

10 9 8 7 6 5 4 3 2 11 12 13 14 15

PRINTED IN SINGAPORE 46
FIRST EDITION, JULY 2011

THE DISPLAY TYPE WAS HAND-LETTERED AS WELL AS SET IN SPELLSTONE AND FORKBEARD CONDENSED.
THE TEXT WAS SET IN CC ASTRO CITY.
THE ART WAS CREATED USING PENCIL SKETCHES AND PHOTOSHOP.
BOOK DESIGN BY TEDD ARNOLD AND LILLIE HOWARD

by STEVE METZGER

illustrated by TEDD ARNOLD

ORCHARD BOOKS/NEW YORK
AN IMPRINT OF SCHOLASTIC INC.

To Stan Freberg
—S.M.

For Matt McElligott,
artiste extraordinaire!
—T.A.

MY NAME IS BLUE – *DETECTIVE* BLUE. YOU MIGHT KNOW ME AS LITTLE BOY BLUE.
THINGS TO DO TODAY:
REPORT OF PORRIDGE SMELLS IN

AT ONE TIME I BLEW A HORN AND LOOKED AFTER COWS AND SHEEP.
THAT'S IN THE *PAST!*
HEY, BLUE,
GOOD LUCK WITH YOUR NEW JOB! DON'T FORGET YOUR OLD PALS—
COWS & SHEEP

THE QUEEN'S TARTS
HOT CROSS BUNS
BLUE DETECTIVE AGENCY
TODAY STARTED LIKE ANY OTHER DAY.
THE *DISH* RAN AWAY WITH THE *SPOON*.

I CLEANED UP *THAT* SITUATION IN TIME FOR LUNCH!
WE'RE ALL *WASHED UP* NOW!

MARY'S LAMB ALMOST MADE IT INTO THE SCHOOLHOUSE.
DILLER SCHOOL

I SEE THROUGH YOUR DISGUISE!

YOU CAN'T PULL THE WOOL OVER MY EYES!
A TEN O'CLOCK SCHOLAR!
HE FOLLOWS ME EVERYWHERE!
HOW WILL I LEARN TO READ?

SUDDENLY I SAW JACK SPRAT *RUNNING* DOWN THE STREET. I THOUGHT SOMEONE HAD OFFERED HIM A FATTY SANDWICH.

HE WAS *SHOUTING!*
MISS MUFFET IS *MISSING!* MISS MUFFET IS *MISSING!*
SPRAT'S SPROUTS
DO YOU KNOW THE MUFFIN MAN?
HE LIVES ON DRURY LANE.

WHAT'S GOING ON, SPRAT?

MISS MUFFET IS MISSING! SHE MIGHT BE IN DANGER!

DON'T WORRY. DETECTIVE BLUE IS ON THE CASE!

I WENT TO THE SCENE OF THE *CRIME* AND SNOOPED AROUND.

LITTLE BO PEEP WAS NEARBY.
MAYBE *SHE* KNEW SOMETHING.
HERE, SHEEPY SHEEPY *SHEEP!*
TODAY SHEEPSHEARING WORKSHOP

EXCUSE ME, BO PEEP. DO YOU KNOW WHERE I CAN FIND MISS MUFFET? SHE'S *MISSING!*

SHE'S NOT ALL THAT'S MISSING. I'VE LOST MY SHEEP!

AND I DON'T KNOW WHERE TO FIND THEM.

MAYBE IF YOU LEAVE THEM ALONE, THEY'LL COME HOME.

THAT'S SILLY.
SNIP

I WAS GETTING NOWHERE, FAST!
MAYBE HUMPTY DUMPTY SAW SOMETHING. HE'S A GOOD EGG.
MILLY! BECKY! WHERE ARE YOU?
I HATE HAIRCUT DAY!
CACKLE, CACKLE!

I CLIMBED TO THE TOP OF HUMPTY DUMPTY'S WALL.
SING A SONG OF SIXPENCE
TONIGHT! CONCERT IN THE CASTLE

DUMPTY SAID HE DOZED OFF WHILE HE WAS *TANNING.*
I WAS SO *PALE!*
HE DID *NOT* SEE MISS MUFFET.

DUMPTY MENTIONED THAT SOMETIMES MUFFET VISITS *LITTLE JACK HORNER*.
SHE LOVES HIS PIES!

THAT'S A **GREAT** TIP!

I SLAPPED DUMPTY ON THE BACK.

OOPS! I GUESS THAT WAS A MISTAKE. I CALLED ALL THE KING'S HORSES AND ALL THE KING'S MEN.
KRUNCH!

NOW LET'S SEE WHAT JACK HORNER HAS TO SAY!
WHO JUST RAN BY?
I DIDN'T SEE ANYONE.
MAYBE IT WAS THE FARMER'S WIFE.

HERE'S THE ***STRANGE*** PART. WHEN I ASKED HIM ABOUT MISS MUFFET, HE ***THUMBED*** A PLUM AND SAID...

FORGET THE PLUM, HORNER!

JUST GIVE ME THE FACTS!

SHE HASN'T BEEN HERE TODAY. YOU MIGHT TRY OLD KING COLE'S CASTLE. SHE LIKES HIS MERRY OLD MUSIC.
PUDDIN' AND PIE, PLEASE!
GEORGIE PORGIE

TIME WAS RUNNING OUT! I *RAN* TO THE CASTLE.
FREE CONCERT

IT WAS *LOUD!* OLD KING COLE'S FIDDLERS PLAYED "HICKORY DICKORY ROCK."

JACK BE NIMBLE AMAZED *EVERYONE* WITH HIS CANDLE-STICK JUMPING.

IN THE CASTLE

I ASKED OLD MOTHER HUBBARD AND SIMPLE SIMON ABOUT ***MUFFET***.

NOTHING! ***NADA!*** THAT'S WHEN I NOTICED A SPIDER.

HEY, SPIDER! IT WAS YOUR WEB NEXT TO MISS MUFFET'S TUFFET.

DID YOU FRIGHTEN HER AWAY?

NO! SHE WAS TIRED OF CURDS AND WHEY. I TOLD HER WHERE SHE COULD GET DELICIOUS PORRIDGE. NEXT THING I KNEW, SHE WAS GONE!

REPORT OF PORRIDGE SMELLS IN THE WOODS
PORRIDGE! THANKS, SPIDER.

I KNEW JUST ONE PLACE FOR PORRIDGE, AND THAT MEANT MUFFET WAS IN DANGER! I FOLLOWED MY NOSE TO A HOUSE IN THE WOODS.

BEARS! RUN FOR YOUR LIFE!
OOF!
SOMEONE'S BEEN EATING MY PORRIDGE!

HALT! THE BEARS ARE NOT FOLLOWING YOU.

ARE YOU MISS MUFFET?
YES. I'M MISS GOLDILOCKS MUFFET.

SHE SPILLED THE BEANS ABOUT HATING CURDS AND WHEY.
I REALLY LOVE PORRIDGE! I'M SORRY ABOUT THE BROKEN CHAIR AND EVERYTHING.

BACK AT COLE'S CASTLE, EVERYONE CELEBRATED THE SAFE RETURN OF MISS GOLDILOCKS MUFFET!

MISS MUFFET IS MISSING
CASE CLOSED